For Nel, the best hugger in the Jenkins family! – M.S.

For my loving parents – M.F.

ORCHARD BOOKS

First published in Great Britain in 2018 by The Watts Publishing Group

1 3 5 7 9 10 8 6 4 2

Text © Mark Sperring 2018

Illustrations © Maddie Frost 2018

The moral rights of the author and illustrator have been asserted.

A CIP catalogue record for this book is available from the British Library.

ISBN 978 1 408 36523 6

Printed and bound in China

Orchard Books
An imprint of Hachette Children's Group
Part of The Watts Publishing Group Limited
Carmelite House, 50 Victoria Embankment, London EC4Y 0DZ

Hachette Ireland
8 Castlecourt, Castleknock, Dublin 15, Ireland

An Hachette UK Company
www.hachette.co.uk   www.hachettechildrens.co.uk

The Littlest Things give the Loveliest Hugs

Mark Sperring and Maddie Frost

ORCHARD

How do you do it, my sweet beetle bug?
You're ever so clever at giving a hug . . .

You snuggle so nicely, it really is true . . .

Nobody, nowhere, can **cuddle like you!**

When we cosy up in our sweet comfy nest,
You're so squishy-squashy,
You're simply the best!

There's something about you
that's perfectly snug . . .

Yes, the littlest things give the
loveliest hugs!

So come here this instant,
my duckling, my dear.
Just waddle up to me,
I need you right here.

Show me that
wonderful thing
that you do . . .

For nobody,
nowhere, can
cuddle
like you!

You must have learnt hugging
from small fluffy things,
with fur soft as velvet
or white downy wings.

Your hugs are a triumph,
my darling, my dove,

For the littlest things give the
loveliest hugs!

So, down in our burrow, we'll cosy up close.
With leaves wrapped around us . . .

we're warmer than toast.
I'll sing to you softly . . .

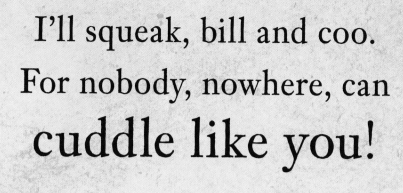

I'll squeak, bill and coo.
For nobody, nowhere, can
cuddle like you!

And mummies and daddies
throughout the land,
We know that it's true –
yes, we all understand . . .

That nestled in burrows or curled under rugs . . .

The littlest things give
the loveliest hugs!